Jack
and the
Beanstalk

JOSEPHINE POOLE

PAUL HESS

*Hodder
Children's
Books*

A division of Hodder Headline Limited

First published in Great Britain in 1997
by Macdonald Young Books

This edition first published in 2004 by Hodder Children's Books
a division of Hodder Headline Limited
338 Euston Road London NW1 3BH

British Library Cataloguing in Publication Data
A catalogue record of this book is available from the British Library.

ISBN 0 340 87784 7 (PB)

10 9 8 7 6 5 4 3 2

Printed in China

Once there was a boy called Jack. He was brave and cheerful, but he was dreadfully spoilt, because his mother was a widow and he was her only child. She gave him everything he wanted, until she had nothing left but her cottage and a cow.

"Alas!" she exclaimed one day. "Jack, my poor boy – look here!" She opened the food cupboard, and the startled Jack saw that it was empty!

"I must sell the cow," she sobbed. "She's a faithful animal, but we can't starve!"

"Cheer up, Mother!" cried Jack. "I'll find a farmer who'll give her a good home – and us a good price as well!"

He hugged her, and she wiped her eyes. Surely he was the best boy in the world!

Jack walked off with the cow. Presently he saw a man coming towards him.

"That's a fine cow," he said.

"She's for sale," said Jack.

"How much?"

"Twenty pounds!" It was a lot of money
in those days.

"Twenty pounds – and I dare say
she's worth every penny. But I'll do better
than that!"

He emptied his purse into Jack's hand.
Jack stared. "Beans!" he exclaimed
in disgust.

"*Magic* beans!" said the stranger. "I wouldn't part with them for anything, except I like the look of you. Scatter them, and they'll make your fortune!"

The beans were large and pink, with black spots. Jack turned them over, wondering. The stranger took the cow.

"What will my mother say?" Jack shouted after him.

"Never fear! You won't regret it!"

Jack ran home, feeling excited. He shouted for his mother. "Look what I've got!" He held out his handful of beans.

She turned pale, and her mouth opened wide with dismay. Then she screamed, "What have you done? Is that all you got for my precious cow?"

"But they're *magic* beans, Mother!"

"Magic! You fool!" He had never seen her so angry. She slapped the beans out of his hand, scattering them over the garden. Then she burst into tears. "Oh, woe! What will become of us now?"

When Jack woke next morning, his tiny room was still dark. He ran to the window.

A mat of green leaves covered the glass!

He dashed outside, and saw a gigantic bean plant. It climbed up – up – like a ladder into the sky!

He tried his weight on the stalk. It was strong and springy. His mother looked out.

"What's this? Jack! What are you doing?"

"Those beans were magic after all! I'm going to seek my fortune!"

"No! Come back at once!"

"I will – with a bag full of gold!"

She couldn't stop him. Up he climbed – hand after hand, foot after foot. Soon he was out of sight.

J ack climbed, and climbed. At last he reached the top, and stepped into a bleak, barren land – nothing but dry earth and stones. He sat down on a boulder, full of gloom. What fortune could there be in this dismal place?

Then he saw an aged crone hobbling towards him. She called out, "Jack!"

How did she know his name? He got up to meet her. She grasped his sleeve with her skinny hand.

"Here you are at last! I've been waiting for you. Do you know what happened to your father?"

"He died when I was a baby," said Jack, tears springing to his eyes.

"He was murdered, Jack – by a giant, who stole everything he owned. That monster built himself a castle and filled it with your father's treasures!"

"Where is he?" cried Jack furiously.

"Find him, before he finds you!" With these cautionary words, the old woman vanished.

As Jack stared around he noticed huge footprints in the earth. He followed them with a beating heart.

At last a grim castle loomed in the distance. A woman sat outside, fanning herself. As he approached, she shouted, "Go away, boy! My husband will be home directly!"

"Oh please, won't you give me a drink? I'm so thirsty!"

"Hurry, then! If he catches you, he'll gobble you up!"

She led him inside. As the castle door slammed behind them, Jack's heart turned cold with dread.

A cauldron bubbled on the kitchen fire, but the woman gave him milk and cake. He had just finished when a tremendous voice boomed at the castle gate.

"FEE, FIE, FO, FUM! I SMELL
THE BLOOD OF AN ENGLISHMAN!"

The outside door crashed open.

"Quick!" hissed the woman in a panic.
She opened the cold oven and Jack jumped
inside. Next instant, the floor shuddered
under a mighty tread. The Giant roared,

"BE HE ALIVE OR BE HE DEAD, I'LL
GRIND HIS BONES TO MAKE MY BREAD!"

The oven was black as night. Trembling
all over, Jack peeped through the crack
between the hinges.

He saw a huge and hideous giant lurching to the table!

"What's for supper, Wife? Shall I fetch it from the oven?"

"No, no! Here you are!" She ladled his helping out of the cauldron. It was so heavy, she had to carry it with both hands.

15

When the Giant had eaten the stew, and drunk a whole barrel of wine, he seemed contented. He settled back in his chair.

"Wife!" he rumbled, in a voice like thunder. "Before you go to bed, get me my hen!"

The wife ran off, and came back with a basket. A hen sat inside.

"Lay!" growled the Giant.

Jack watched in amazement. Every time the Giant said, "Lay!" the hen laid an egg of solid gold!

Here was treasure!

Now the Giant was getting sleepy. His head began to nod.

Jack undid the oven and opened the door a fraction. The Giant never moved. Jack slipped quietly, quietly to the ground. The Giant started to snore. Jack stole to the table. He lifted the basket carefully – and then he sped away.

Jack dashed to the castle door. Alas! It was bolted and barred and he couldn't open it. But he spied a little window, unfastened. He crept through and pulled the basket after him. Then – he was off like the wind!

He shinned down the beanstalk, balancing the basket. His unhappy mother was still waiting in the garden, certain that he had come to a miserable end.

Oh, joy! Now their troubles were over. They had only to say, "Lay!" and the obedient hen produced a golden egg. The cottage glowed with happiness.

But Jack couldn't forgive the Giant, that murderer and thief. The beanstalk still grew in the cottage garden, for he wouldn't let his mother cut it down. He meant to climb it again – but he didn't tell her that.

One day when his mother was out visiting, Jack took his chance and climbed the beanstalk. He had grown since last time, and he was smartly dressed. He wore his mother's spectacles as well, not wanting to be recognized.

When he reached the top he was very tired indeed, and it seemed a long, long way to the Giant's castle.

The Giant's wife sat outside, plucking a chicken.

"Madam," said Jack, bowing low, "I beg you to shelter me for the night, for I have lost my way."

"Never!" cried she. "The last time I took pity on a boy, he stole the magic hen, and my husband has blamed me for it ever since!"

Jack was sorry about this. However, he persuaded her at last, and she took him into the kitchen and fed him. He dawdled there until he heard the Giant roar at the castle gate.

"FEE, FIE, FO, FUM! I SMELL
THE BLOOD OF AN ENGLISHMAN!
BE HE ALIVE OR BE HE DEAD, I'LL
GRIND HIS BONES TO MAKE MY BREAD!"

Then the frantic wife hid Jack in the boot cupboard, and the Giant came storming into the kitchen.

That night the Giant stuffed himself with roast meat, potatoes and wine. When he was satisfied, he shouted at his wife to bring him his hoards of gold and silver before she went to bed.

Jack peeped out through the keyhole. He had never seen so much money! He watched while the Giant counted it lovingly into bags and tied it up tight. Then, at last, his huge head lolled and he started to snore.

Jack crept up to the table. Suddenly, a little dog darted out from under the chair and began to bark! Quick as lightning, he tossed it a scrap of meat from the Giant's plate.

He grabbed the bags and dashed from the room. He crammed himself and the money through the little window, and ran at top speed to the beanstalk and safety. He dropped the bags first, and scrambled down. There stood his mother, laughing and clapping her hands, for the garden was covered with gold and silver coins!

Now Jack's mother forbade him to climb the beanstalk. She was sure he would come to grief, and that would be the end of their happiness.

But he couldn't forget how the Giant had treated his father. He meant to outwit him once more.

On Midsummer day he got up very early while his mother was still asleep. He dyed his face and hands, chopped off his curls and dressed in rags. Then he began to climb. The beanstalk seemed taller than ever. The castle seemed even further away, and by the time he reached it he was exhausted. The Giant's wife was sitting outside, shelling peas. He begged for a drink.

"Not for the crown of England!" she cried. "My life has been unbearable since last I took in a stranger, for he stole all my husband's money!"

But Jack looked so wretched, and pleaded so hard, that at last she led him into the kitchen.

"FEE, FIE, FO, FUM! I SMELL THE BLOOD OF AN ENGLISHMAN! BE HE ALIVE OR BE HE DEAD, I'LL GRIND HIS BONES TO MAKE MY BREAD!"

"Home already!" cried the terrified wife. "Quick! In here!" She bundled Jack into the copper. It was used for boiling the Giant's dirty clothes, so there was plenty of room inside.

This time the Giant was quite sure that he could smell human blood. He searched the kitchen – he even put his huge hand on the copper! But his wife managed to distract him with his supper. Three whole deer he ate, cracking the bones and hurling them on the floor, and pulling out the bung of the wine barrel with his teeth!

When he had finished, the Giant roared for his harp. Jack peeped out under the lid of the copper. He saw the wife bring in the golden instrument, before she retired upstairs.

"Play," mumbled the Giant. At once the magic harp vibrated with the most thrilling music, with never a touch from the Giant.

Jack listened, enchanted. This
was the finest treasure of them all!

As soon as the Giant started
to snore, he slipped out of
the copper. He glided
to the table and laid
his hand on the golden
harp. But, oh! Instantly
it wailed, "Master!
Master!"

Jack was dreadfully frightened, but he meant to keep the harp. He held it tightly, and dashed out of the kitchen. He could hear the Giant stumbling about, and hoped he was too drunk to run fast. The little window was still unfastened. He crept through, and sped away. But the cool night air cleared the Giant's head, and soon Jack heard the regular THUMP THUMP of his great feet behind him.

Jack ran like the wind, with the harp crying, "Master! Master!" The shadow of the Giant fell over him as he leapt for the beanstalk. He flung himself down from branch to branch, jumping the last distance.

He set the harp on the cottage table, and
shouted at his mother to stay indoors. He
snatched the axe he used for chopping
firewood. Then he struck, again and again, at
the strong trunk of the beanstalk.

He was only just in time. He could see the wicked Giant's huge feet, fumbling for a foothold. The Giant crashed to the ground and he was so heavy, that the fall killed him.

Now there was no way of getting anything more from the castle. But Jack had saved the best of his father's treasures, and he reckoned the kindly wife deserved to keep what was left. He told his mother the whole story, and after that they lived in perfect happiness.

Other stories to collect and treasure: